Y0-AWI-440

# I'm Glad you're my Dad!

by
Marianne Richmond

# I'm Glad You're my Dad!

© 2005 by Marianne Richmond Studios, Inc.

All rights reserved. No part of this book may be
reproduced or transmitted in any form or by any means,
electronic or mechanical, including photocopying, recording
or any information storage and retrieval system,
without permission in writing from the publisher.

Marianne Richmond Studios, Inc.
420 N. 5th Street, Suite 840
Minneapolis, MN 55401
www.mariannerichmond.com

ISBN 0-9763101-2-0

Illustrations by Marianne Richmond

Book design by Sara Dare Biscan

Printed in China

First Printing

TO Dad
FROM Miriam
Date Sunday June 18, 2006

Dear Dad,

    I think it a lot and probably don't tell you     enough — I'm glad you're my dad!

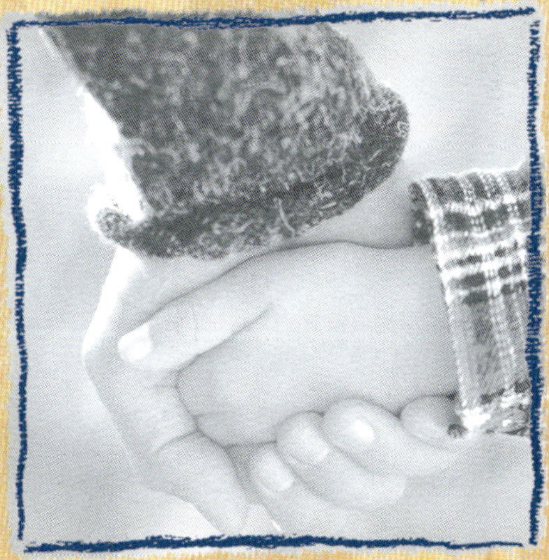

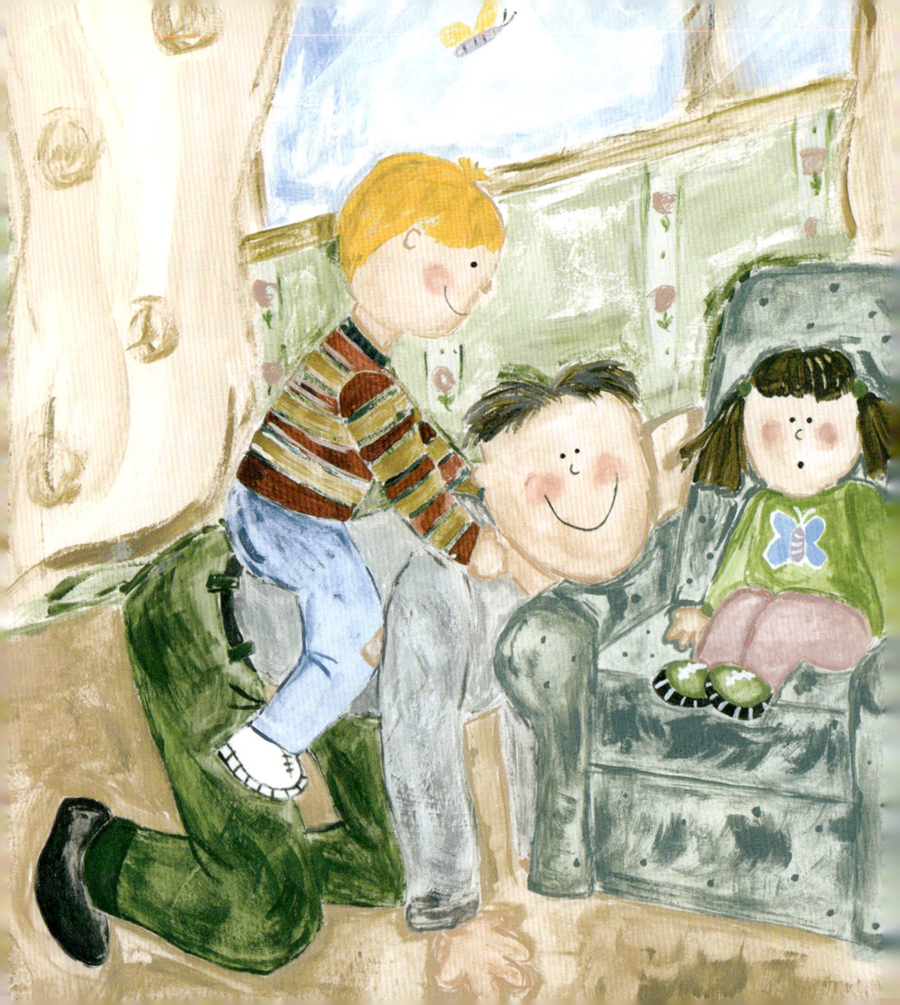

I'm glad you like to play. I like hanging out together... playing ball, games or watching TV.

Thanks for making time for me...

even when
I know
you have
dad things
to do.

I'm glad you're my dad because you make sure our family has enough food and stuff.

Plus — fun things like vacations, eating out, and toys.

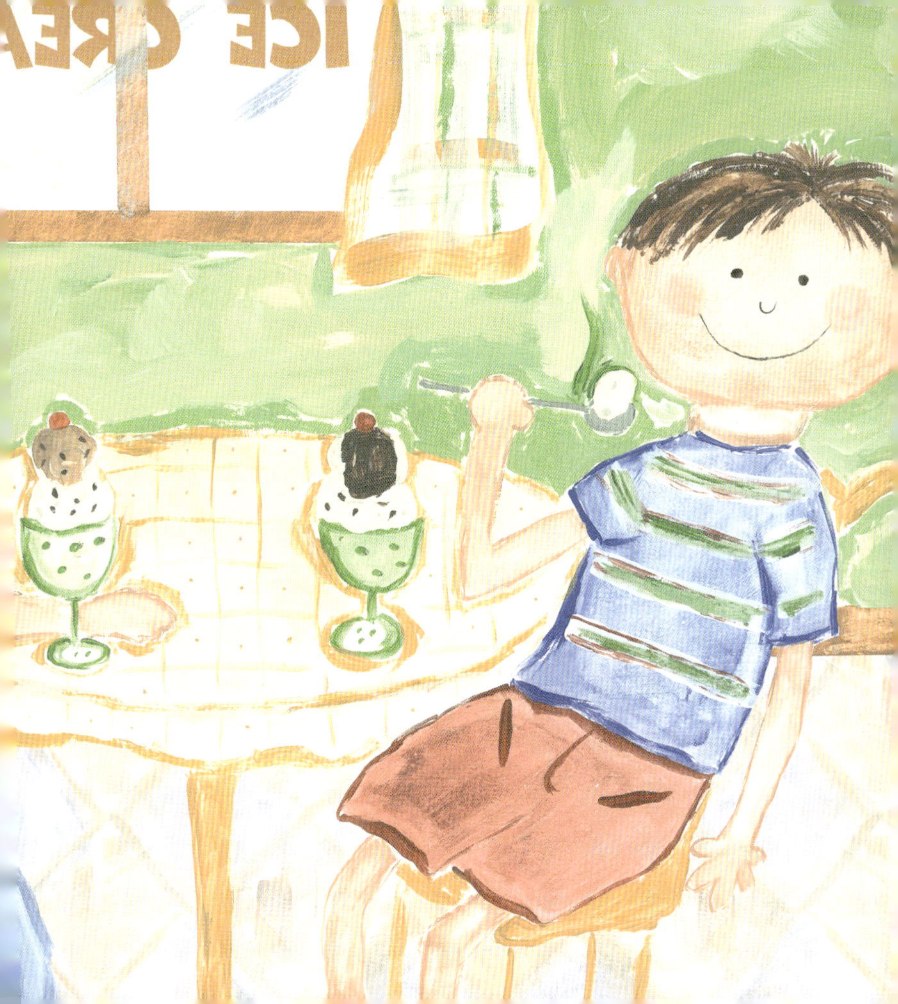
ICE CREA

I'm glad you're
my dad
because
you're strong
and brave
and smart.

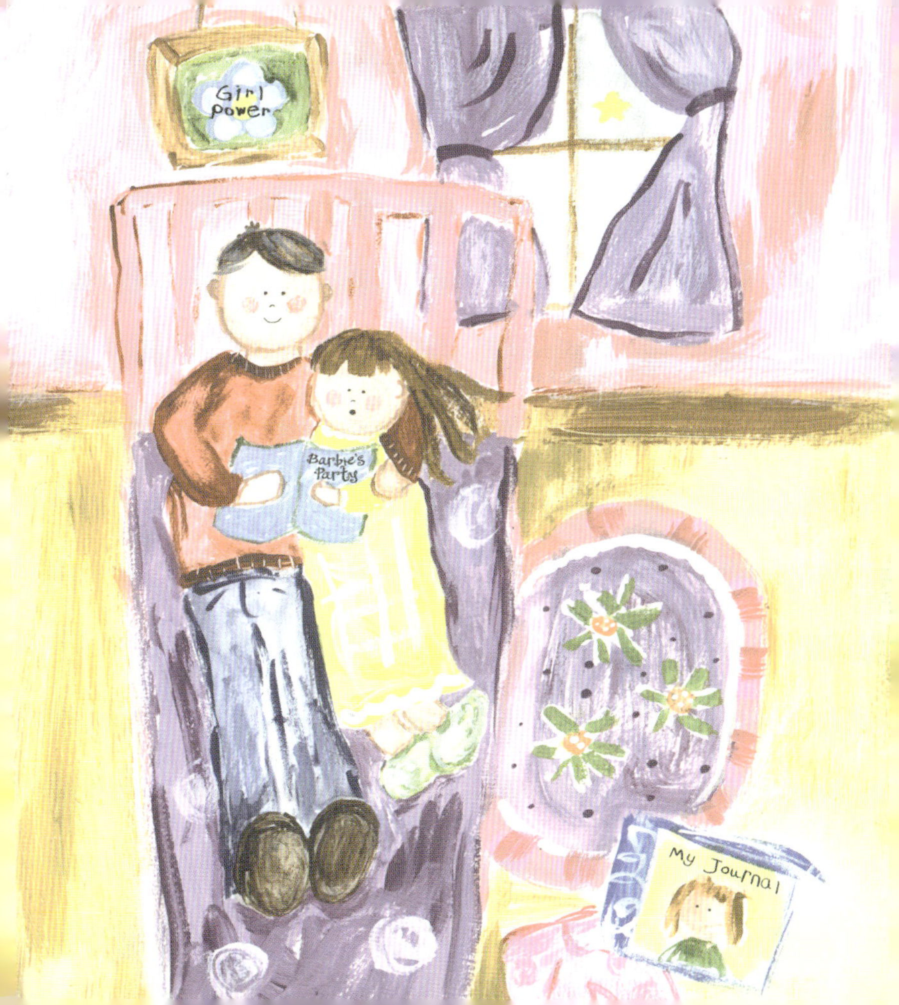
Girl power
Barbie's Party
My Journal

Thanks for helping me with homework, putting things together, replacing batteries, killing bugs, fixing bikes, patching inflatable things...

and making it
look easy.

Thanks, too, for
 your ideas while
we're driving,
 eatin' breakfast,
or brushing teeth.
 I listen even if it
seems like I don't.

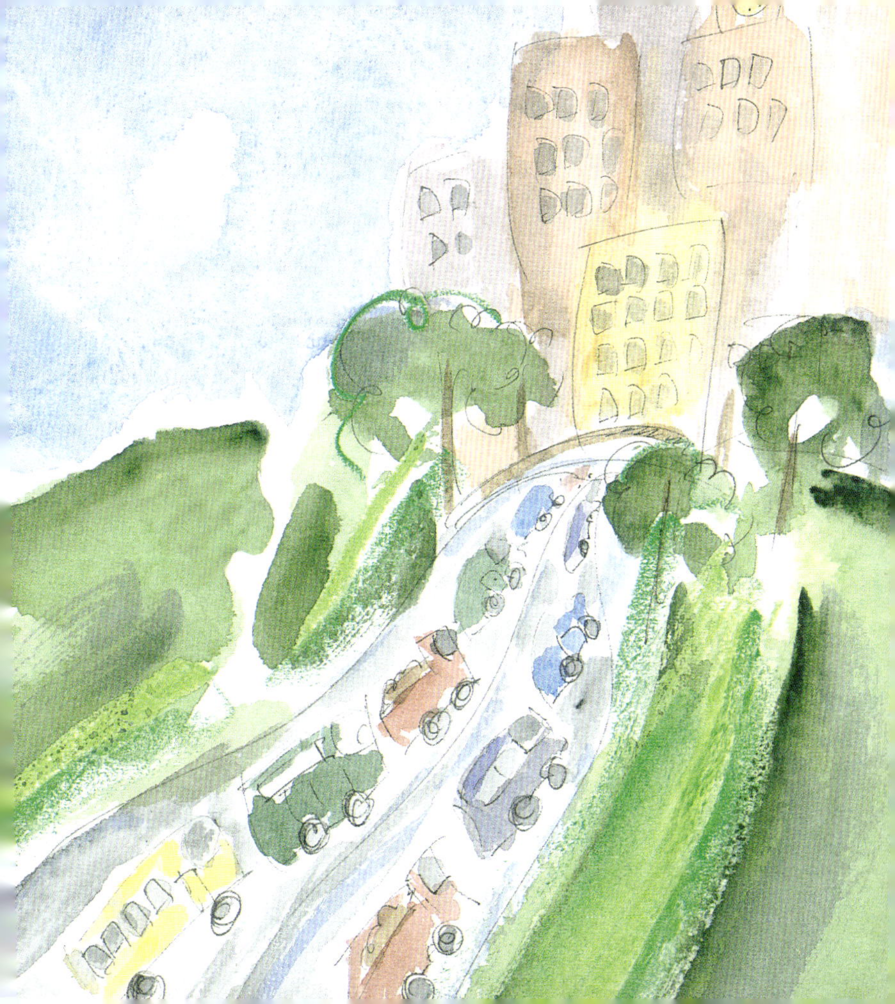

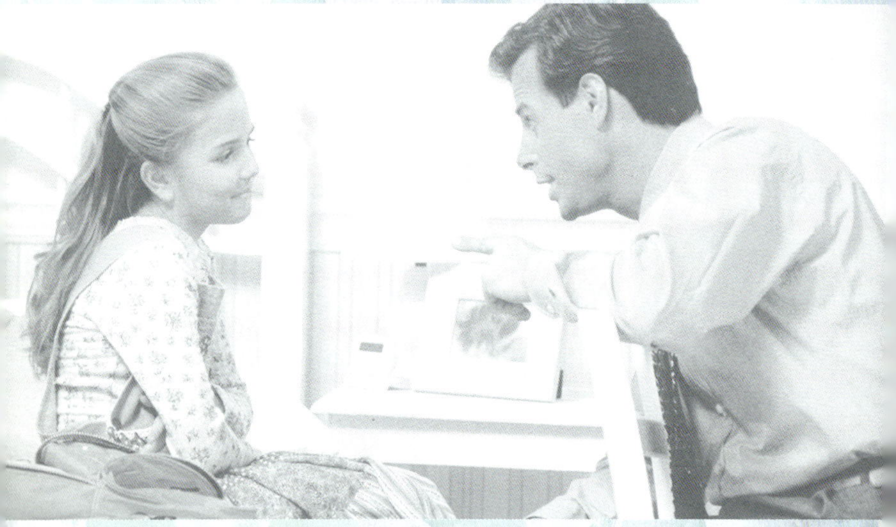

Sometimes I'm <u>not</u> glad about
   your rules and discipline...
but I know you love me.

Thanks for letting
 me figure out
"dad was right"
 instead of saying,
"I told you so..."

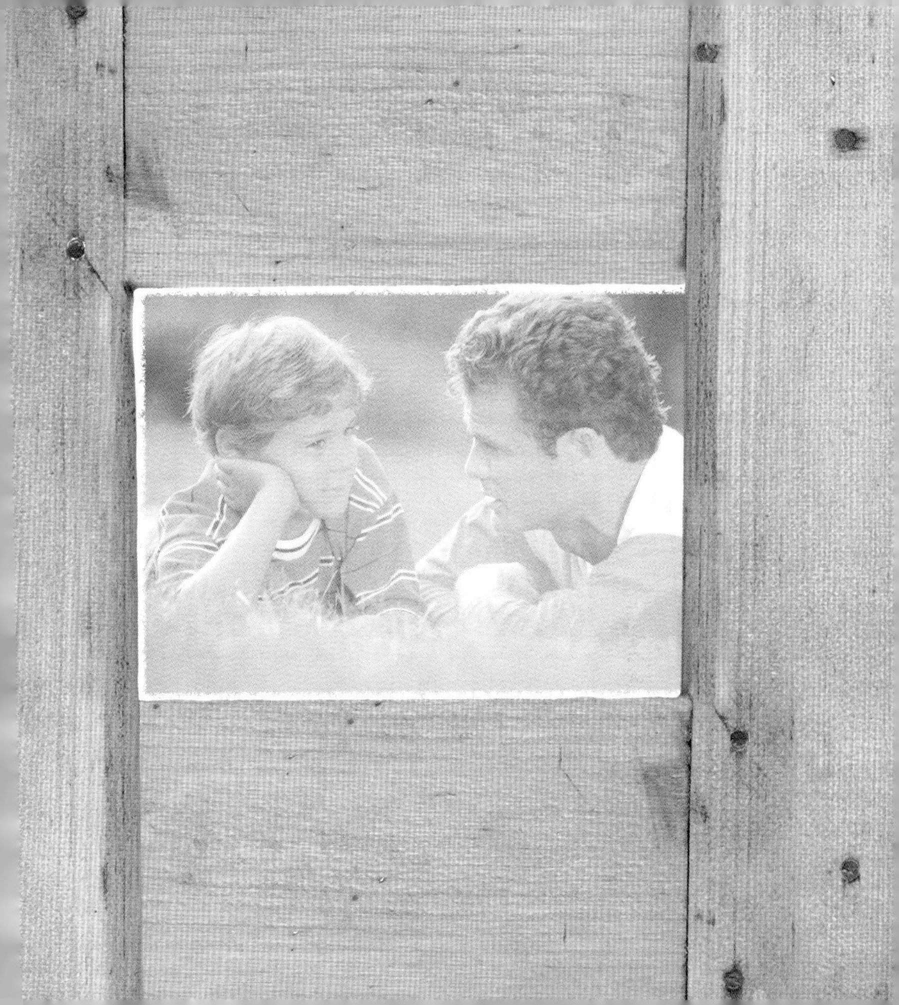

Thanks for _giving_ me your money so I can play a video game, _get_ the cool shoes, or do some kid thing that feels _really_ important to me.

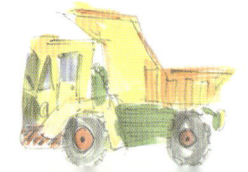

Toy Department

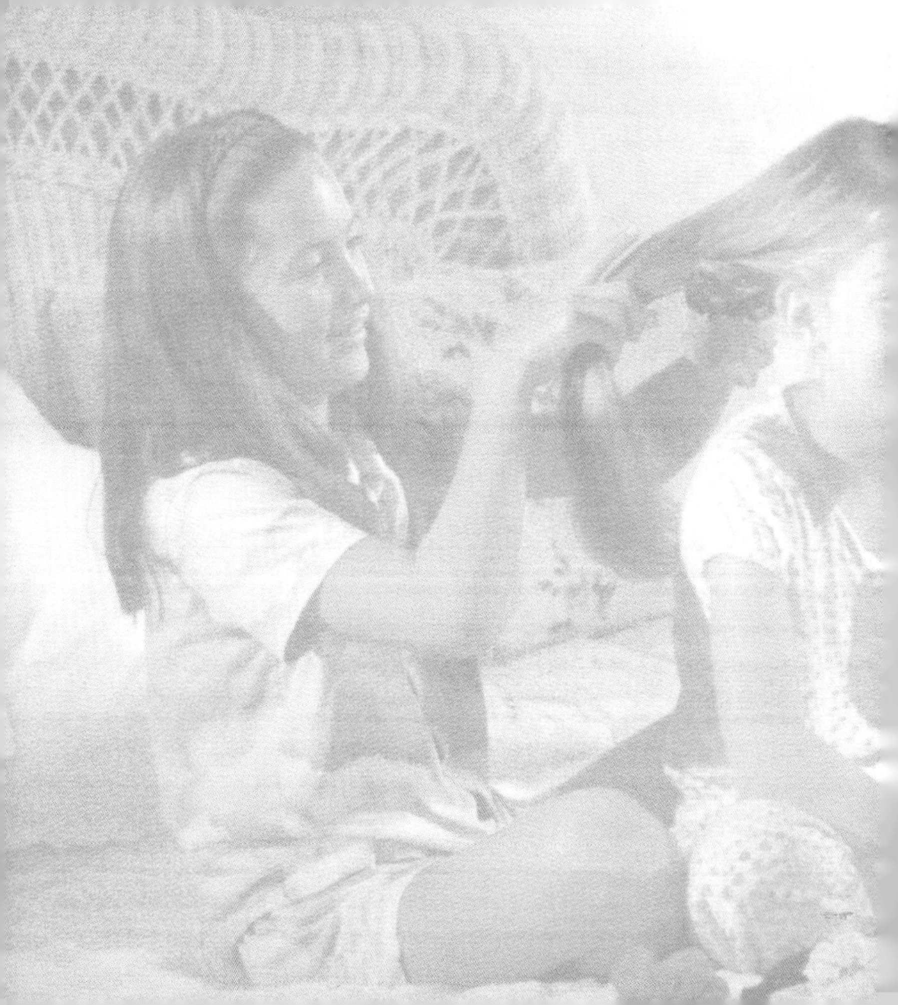

Thanks for
putting up
with my phases...
music, clothes,
haircuts or friends.

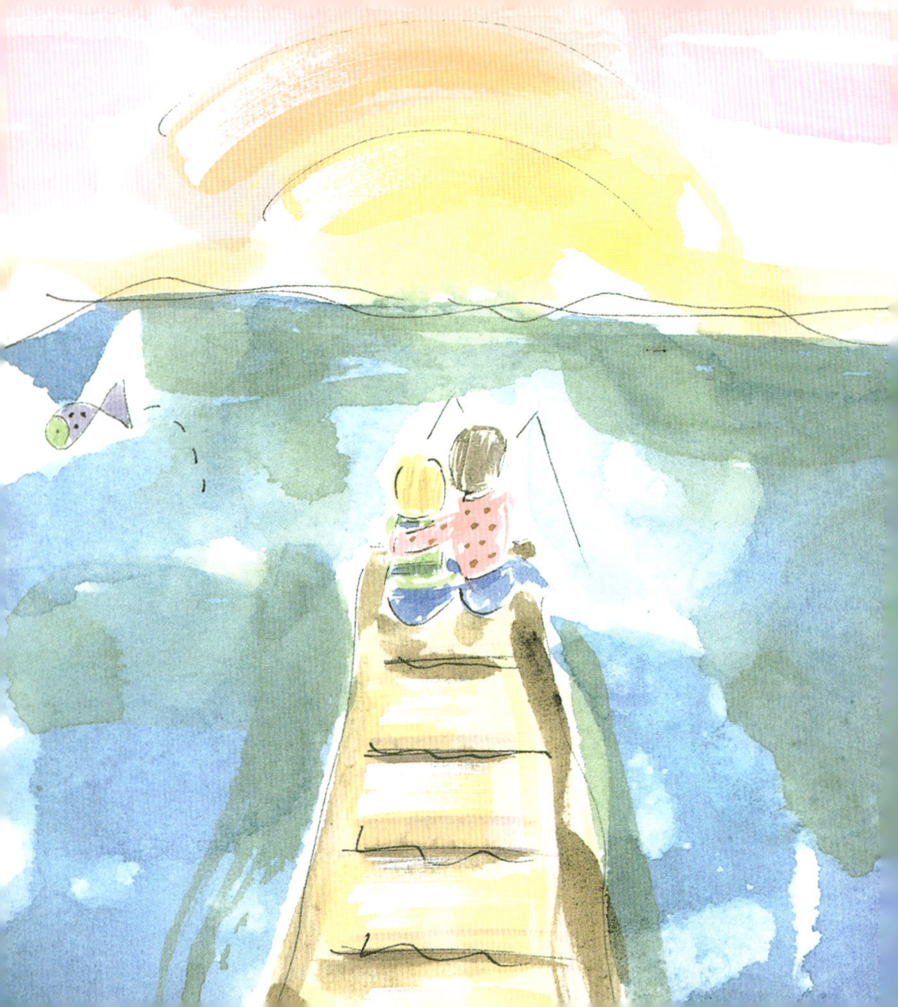

I'm glad you're my dad
   because you tell me to try
new things... especially when you
   know I'll like it. And even
when you know I won't.

Thanks for cheering me on...

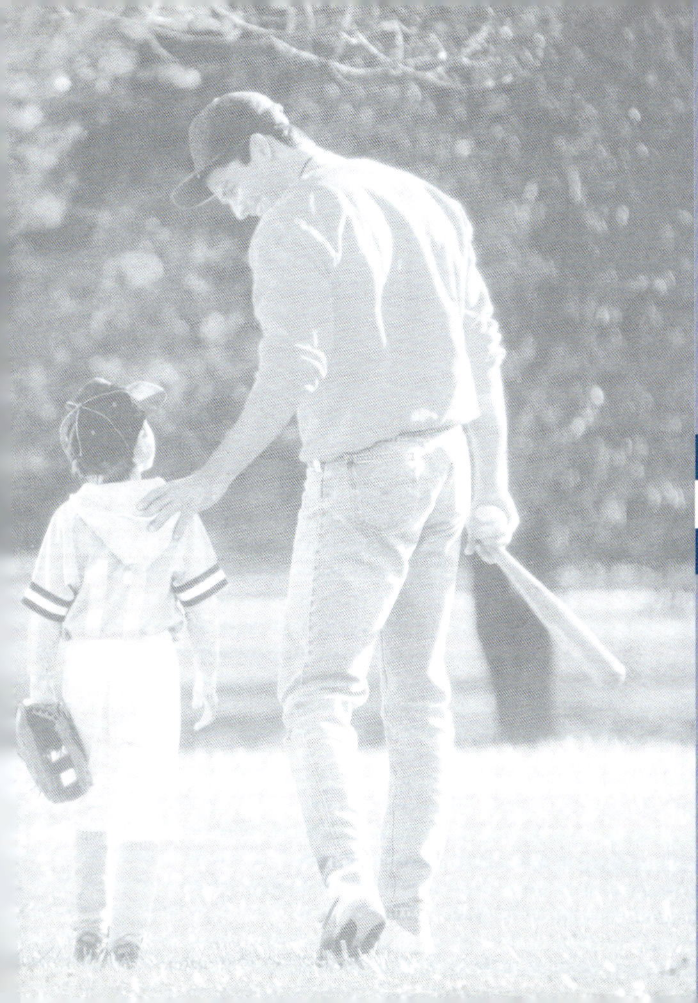

I feel proud when I tell my friends,

"that's my dad."

I'm glad you're my dad because you love me when I'm not very nice.

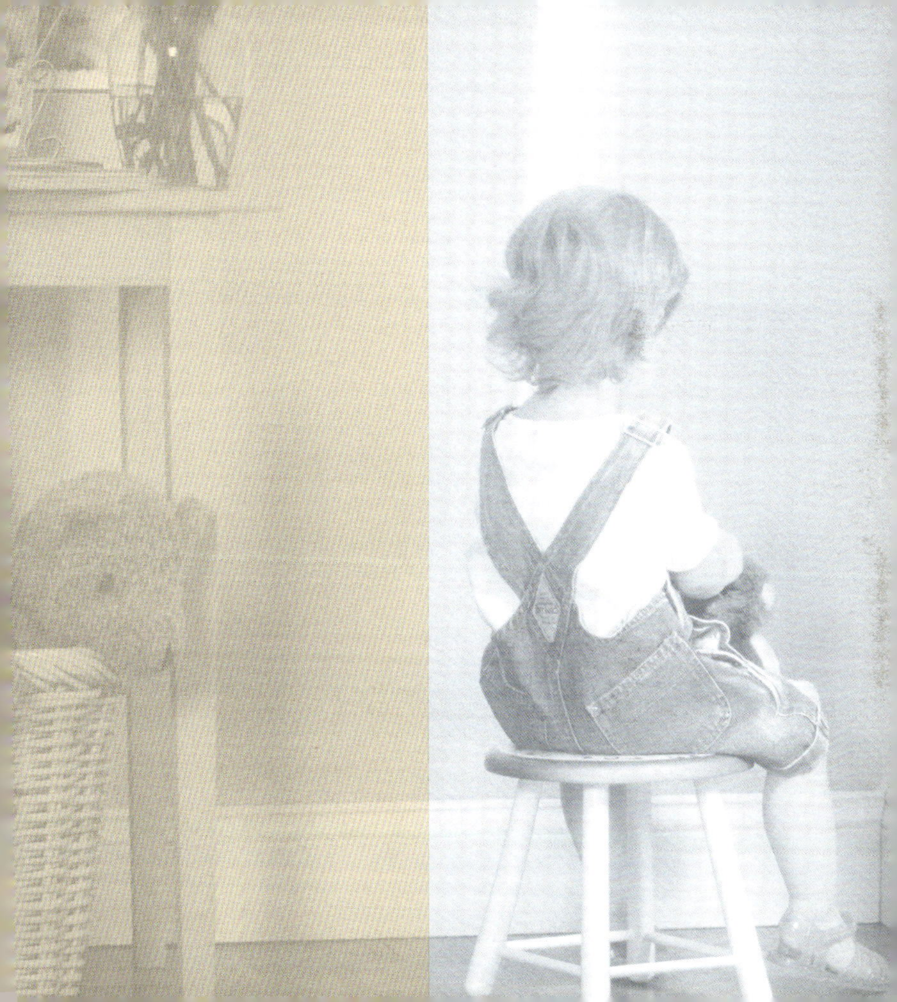

I'm glad you're my dad
 because you can get me
to laugh by tickling me
 or telling me a joke
or by getting me to think
 about something else.

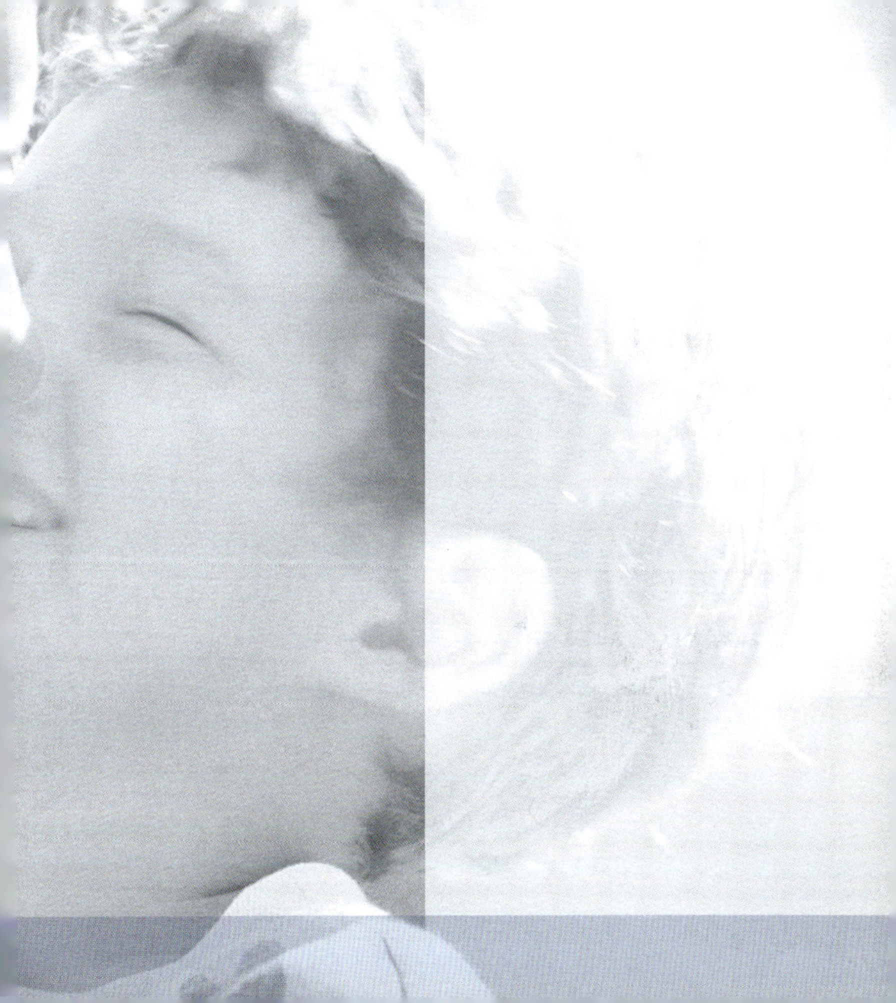

Thanks, dad,
for loving me
day after day.

Thanks for being proud of me, too, and for making me feel special to you.

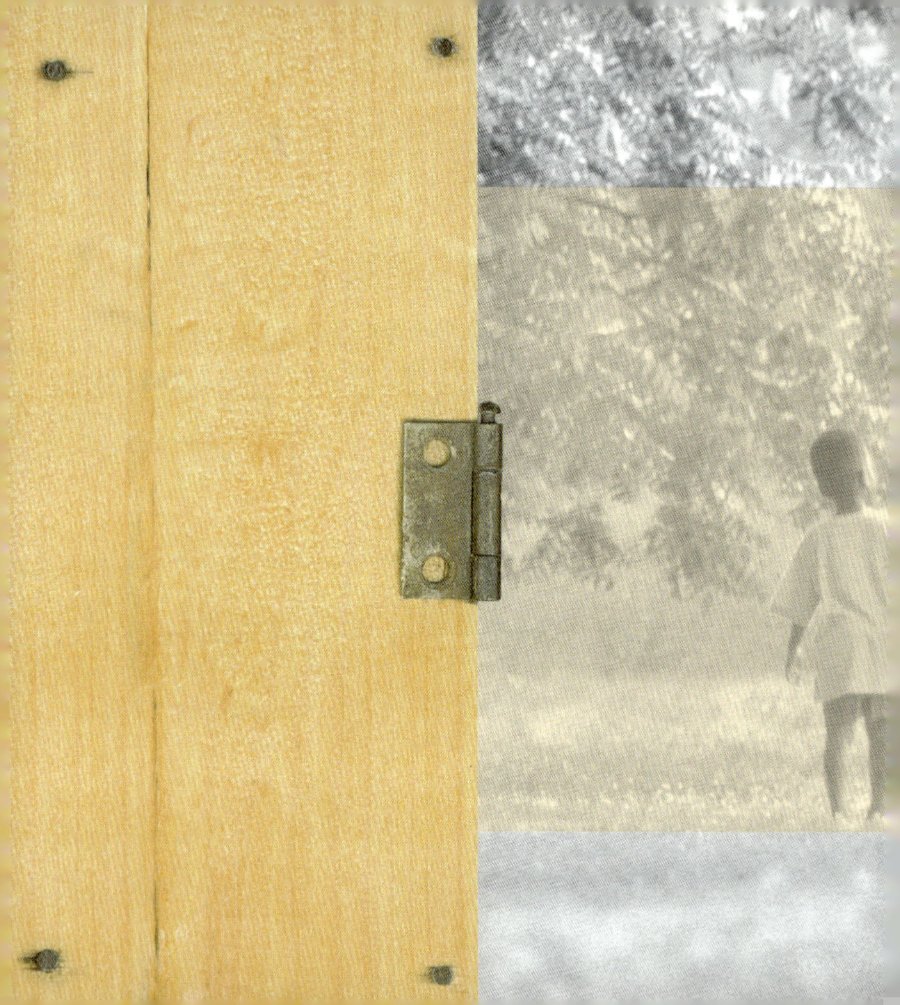

I'm glad
you're
my dad!

A gifted author and artist, Marianne Richmond shares her creations with millions of people worldwide through her delightful books, cards, and giftware. In addition to the *Simply Said...* and *Smartly Said...* gift book series, she has written and illustrated five additional books: **The Gift of an Angel, The Gift of a Memory, Hooray for You!, The Gifts of Being Grand** and **I Love You So....**

To learn more about Marianne's products, please visit www.mariannerichmond.com.